Parent's Introduction

Whether your child is a beginning reader, a reluctant reader, or an eager reader, this book offers a fun and easy way to encourage and help your child in reading.

Developed with reading education specialists, *We Both Read* books invite you and your child to take turns reading aloud. You read the left-hand pages of the book, and your child reads the right-hand pages—which have been written at one of six early reading levels. The result is a wonderful new reading experience and faster reading development!

You may find it helpful to read the entire book aloud yourself the first time, then invite your child to participate the second time. As you read, try to make the story come alive by reading with expression. This will help to model good fluency. It will also be helpful to stop at various points to discuss what you are reading. This will help increase your child's understanding of what is being read.

In some books, a few challenging words are introduced in the parent's text, distinguished with **bold** lettering. Pointing out and discussing these words can help to build your child's reading vocabulary. If your child is a beginning reader, it may be helpful to run a finger under the text as each of you reads. Please also notice that a "talking parent" ☺ icon precedes the parent's text, and a "talking child" ☺ icon precedes the child's text.

If your child struggles with a word, you can encourage "sounding it out," but keep in mind that not all words can be sounded out. Your child might pick up clues about a word from the picture, other words in the sentence, or any rhyming patterns. If your child struggles with a word for more than five seconds, it is usually best to simply say the word.

Most of all, remember to praise your child's efforts and keep the reading fun. After you have finished the book, ask a few questions and discuss what you have read together. Rereading this book multiple times may also be helpful for your child.

Try to keep the tips above in mind as you read together, but don't worry about doing everything right. Simply sharing the enjoyment of reading together will increase your child's reading skills and help to start your child off on a lifetime of reading enjoyment!

The Frog Prince
A We Both Read Book

Published by
Treasure Bay, Inc.
P. O. Box 119
Novato, CA 94948 USA

Printed in Malaysia

Library of Congress Catalog Card Number: 97-62025

Paperback ISBN: 978-1-891327-29-2

Visit us online at:
www.webothread.com

PR-6-16

We Both Read

The Frog Prince

Adapted by Sindy McKay

From the story by the Brothers Grimm

Illustrated by George Ulrich

TREASURE BAY

Long ago, there lived a young **princess** with **golden** hair, who was so beautiful that the sun would smile whenever it saw her. Often, the **princess** would smile back. But sometimes she would shout, "Stop being so hot!"

You see, while this **princess** was usually very nice, sometimes she was not as friendly as she could be.

One day, the king gave the **princess** a ball.

It was a **golden** ball.

She loved her new ball.

She played with it every day.

     One warm and sunny afternoon, the princess took her golden ball and wandered into the nearby forest, a place she had promised never to go. She began to play, tossing the ball into the air and catching it in her hand.

The ball went up.

The ball came down.

Up and down. Up and down.

And then . . . she missed.

Plunk! The ball fell to the ground.

Splash! It rolled into a nearby spring.

Glug! It sank into the cold, **deep** water.

"Oh, no!" cried the princess.

She looked into the **deep** water.

But she could not see her golden ball.

The golden ball was gone.

The princess began to cry. Louder and louder she wailed! Suddenly, a raspy voice called out, "Excuse me, Princess. Is something wrong?"

There in the spring, with its big **head** stretching out of the water and its thin **arms** reaching over the rim, was a frog.

The princess jumped back.

She did not like big **heads**.

She did not like thin **arms**.

She did not like frogs.

Being very careful not to get too close, the princess told the frog that she had lost her ball in the spring.

The frog smiled and politely told her, "I'm a very good swimmer. I would be happy to swim down and **find** your ball for you."

The princess still did not like frogs.

But maybe this frog was not so bad.

Maybe this frog could **find** her golden ball.

"Can you really bring back my golden ball to me?" the princess asked hopefully.

"I can indeed," **replied** the **friendly** frog. "Then perhaps you can do a favor for me," he added.

"What would you like?" asked the princess in surprise.

The frog **replied**, "I want to eat with you.

I want to sleep on your pillow.

I want to be your **friend.**"

Now the princess did not want to be friends with a frog. But she did want her ball back. So she promised to do what the frog had asked.

However, the princess knew she would never keep her promise.

She thought to herself, "A frog eats bugs.

A frog sleeps near the water.

A frog could never be my friend."

Of course, she did not say any of this to the frog. And the frog did not know that, while a promise is a promise, this princess sometimes made promises she did not keep.

So, with a joyful heart, he dove in to find the missing ball at the **bottom** of the spring.

Down, down, down, he went to the **bottom**.

Up, up, up, he came to the top.

And the golden ball came up with him.

The frog proudly dropped the ball at the feet of the delighted princess, and she quickly scooped it up and merrily skipped away. She did not even thank the frog. And she certainly did not intend to be his friend.

 "Wait!" said the frog. "Please, come back!"

But the princess did not come back.

So the sad frog jumped back into the spring.

　The next evening, the princess was eating dinner with her father, the king, when they heard a strange sound—plitch, plotch, plitch, plotch.

Something was climbing the palace stairs.

Then a raspy voice called out, "Princess! It's me! Please open the door!"

The princess did not want to open the door.

But her father wanted to see who was there.

So she opened it.

Quickly, she slammed the door shut again.

The king could see that she was frightened. "My child, what is it? Who is at the door? Is it a big, **mean monster**?"

The princess shook her head and replied, …

"It is not big.

It is not **mean**.

It is not a **monster**.

It is just a silly old frog."

The king was puzzled by the appearance of a frog at the castle door.

So, the princess explained how the frog had retrieved her golden ball from the spring, and how she had made him a **promise** in exchange for his kindness.

"And what did you **promise**?" asked the king.

"I **promised** he could eat with me.

I **promised** he could sleep on my pillow.

I **promised** I would be his friend.

But I will not!"

The king was shocked. "Dear Daughter, I have always taught you that a promise is a promise," he told her. "If you said you would be his friend, then you must be his friend!"

So, the princess opened the door and allowed the frog to hop in.

The frog asked to eat with the princess.

He asked to sleep on her pillow.

He asked to be her friend.

The princess was filled with dread.

How could she let this slimy frog sit beside her? How could she watch him eat with his long, sticky tongue? How could she let this goggle-eyed creature sleep on her pillow?

How could she ever let a frog be her friend?

She could not do it!

She would not do it!

This frog would *never* be her friend!

The king sternly reminded her, "A promise is a promise. And this one you must keep."

The princess pouted. But she knew deep in her heart that her father was right.

So, she let the frog eat with her.
She let him sleep on her pillow.

The frog was nice and polite.
But she did not like it at all.

Early the next morning, when the dark was graying into daylight, the princess heard the frog jump down from her bed and hop away. She hoped he would never come back again.

But he did come back, the very next night.

Again he ate with her.

Again he went to sleep on her pillow.

Again the frog was nice and polite.

And this time the princess did not hate
it so much.

Early the next morning, when the dark was again graying into daylight, the princess again heard the frog jump down from her bed and hop away. She wondered if he would come back again.

And he did come back, the very next night.

Again he ate with her.

Again he went to sleep on her pillow.

Again he was nice and polite.

And this time she kind of liked it.

Early the next morning, the dark was once more graying into daylight as the princess waited to hear the frog jump down from her bed and hop away. As she waited, she found herself hoping that he would come back again that night.

The frog jumped down from her bed.

But this time he did not hop away.

This time was different. This time was magic. The moment his webbed feet touched the floor, the frog was transformed into a handsome young prince!

Now the princess was glad she had let him eat with her.

She was glad she had let him sleep on her pillow.

She was glad the frog was nice and polite.

Most of all, the princess was glad that she had kept her promise to be his friend.

Then, the princess and the frog prince made one more promise to each other. They promised to live happily ever after.

And they did.

After all, a promise is a promise.

If you liked *The Frog Prince*, here is another We Both Read® book you are sure to enjoy!

Jack and the Beanstalk

This lively retelling of the classic story is filled with humor and excitement. Much to his mother's dismay, Jack trades their only cow for five beans. But from these beans grows a magical beanstalk, which Jack climbs up to confront a fearsome giant. Jack must outwit and outrun the giant to reclaim his family's golden treasures!

To see all the We Both Read books that are available,
just go online to **www.webothread.com**.